HOME

WHERE EVERYONE IS

Poems & Songs

Inspired by American Immigrants

—

DEEPAK CHOPRA

KABIR SEHGAL

PAUL AVGERINOS

GRAND CENTRAL
PUBLISHING

NEW YORK   BOSTON

Grand Central Publishing

Hachette Book Group

1290 Avenue of the Americas, New York, NY 10104

grandcentralpublishing.com

twitter.com/grandcentralpub

First Edition: August 2017

Grand Central Publishing is a division of Hachette Book Group, Inc. The Grand Central
Publishing name and logo is a trademark of Hachette Book Group, Inc.

The publisher is not responsible for websites (or their content) that are not owned by
the publisher.

The Hachette Speakers Bureau provides a wide range of authors for speaking events.
To find out more, go to www.hachettespeakersbureau.com or call (866) 376-6591.

Print book interior design by Cindy Joy

Library of Congress Cataloging-in-Publication Data has been applied for.

ISBNs: 978-1-5387-6100-7 (book), 978-1-4789-9897-6 (audiobook, downloadable),
978-1-5387-6099-4 (ebook)

Printed in the United States of America

10 9 8 7 6 5 4 3 2 1

Dedicated to our fathers:
Krishan, Raghbir, and Constantinos

"Home is the place where, when you have
to go there, they have to take you in."

—ROBERT FROST

"Perhaps home is not a place but simply
an irrevocable condition."

—JAMES BALDWIN

"To meditate means to go home to yourself.
Then you know how to take care of the things that
are happening inside you, and you know how to
take care of the things that happen around you."

—THICH NHAT HANH

SONGS

1   HOME   *Inspired by* Raghbir Sehgal

2   BORDER   *Inspired by* Reyna Grande

3   SURVIVOR   *Inspired by* William Jimeno

4   QUEEN   *Inspired by* Celia Cruz

5   RIVER   *Inspired by* Audrey Hepburn

6   WHISPER   *Inspired by* Yo-Yo Ma

7   COMPASS   *Inspired by* Chimamanda Ngozi Adichie

8   CANDLE   *Inspired by* Kahlil Gibran

9   FATHER   *Inspired by* Krishan Chopra

10   ORBIT   *Inspired by* Kalpana Chawla

11   BEYOND   *Inspired by* Alfred Korzybski

12   INFINITY   *Inspired by* Albert Einstein

CONTENTS

INTRODUCTION   1

· ·

BORDER   *Inspired by Reyna Grande*   12

SURVIVOR   *Inspired by William Jimeno*   14

QUEEN   *Inspired by Celia Cruz*   16

VOICE   *Inspired by Joni Mitchell*   18

MOONFLOWER   *Inspired by Carlos Santana*   20

COMPASS   *Inspired by Chimamanda Ngozi Adichie*   21

HANDS   *Inspired by Hend al-Mansour*   23

CANDLE   *Inspired by Kahlil Gibran*   24

LEGEND   *Inspired by Shulamit Ran*   26

ATLANTIC   *Inspired by Ahmet Ertegun*   28

WHISPER   *Inspired by Yo-Yo Ma*   30

HOME   *Inspired by Raghbir Sehgal*   32

FATHER   *Inspired by Krishan Chopra*   34

ODYSSEY   *Inspired by Constantinos Avgerinos*   35

IDENTITY   *Inspired by Huỳnh Sanh Thông*   36

ORBIT   *Inspired by Kalpana Chawla*   38

NEWS   *Inspired by Nikhil Deogun*   39

CITIZEN   *Inspired by Wong Kim Ark*   41

WORDS   *Inspired by Luisa Aguilar Igloria*   43

CINEMA	*Inspired by James Wong Howe*	44
PASSPORT	*Inspired by Fareed Zakaria*	46
FLOORS	*Inspired by I. M. Pei*	48
CAPS	*Inspired by Elizabeth Blackburn*	50
CODEPOET	*Inspired by Sergey Brin*	52
GUARDIAN	*Inspired by Mary Harris "Mother" Jones*	53
ACE	*Inspired by Martina Navratilova*	55
MAGIC	*Inspired by Maria Goeppert-Mayer*	56
FORTRESS	*Inspired by Madeleine Albright*	59
REVOLUTION	*Inspired by Igor Stravinsky*	61
PATRON	*Inspired by Helena Rubinstein*	63
INFINITY	*Inspired by Albert Einstein*	65
RIVER	*Inspired by Audrey Hepburn*	66
RECIPE	*Inspired by Giada Pamela De Laurentiis*	68
BEYOND	*Inspired by Alfred Korzybski*	69

. . . .

BIOGRAPHIES OF IMMIGRANTS	71
BIOGRAPHIES OF ARTISTS	77
CREDITS	79

INTRODUCTION

We wrote these poems to celebrate and honor immigrants. After all, the United States is a country composed of and built by immigrants, and it has been a beacon to those in search of a new life for hundreds of years. It's engraved on a plaque inside the pedestal's lower level at the Statue of Liberty:

> *"Give me your tired, your poor,*
> *Your huddled masses yearning to breathe free,*
> *The wretched refuse of your teeming shore,*
> *Send these, the homeless, tempest-tost to me,*
> *I lift my lamp beside the golden door!"*

Now, in 2017, more than in recent memory, that lamp is shining less brightly than it used to, and the door is closing. Too many of our friends and family members feel like strangers in their own homeland. According to the U.S. Census Bureau, about 13 percent of America's population, or forty million people, are foreign born, and 25 percent of children under the age of eighteen living in families have at least one parent who was born in another country. Immigrants enrich our country with a vast range of skills, talents, ideas, viewpoints, and perspectives. Their cultural and cognitive diversity helps our country move forward with innovations in almost every sector, from medicine and technology to commerce and the arts. Immigrants are a vital source of energy, infusing our nation with an assiduous and relentless work ethic that keeps the United States competitive in the global marketplace.

For these reasons, spurning immigrants and shunning those who are different from us is a troublesome and dangerous development in our beloved country. To be sure, we support keeping America safe and secure and we believe in respecting fair laws, but the tenor of our cultural conversation has turned inhospitable and even hostile toward immigrants. Building a wall isn't just a physical act. It's also a mental and even metaphorical one in which Americans may close themselves off from interacting with those who are different, contrary to the motto of our country *e pluribus unum*, out of many, one, which has come to beautifully describe our melting pot nature. That some people may feel uninvited, unwanted, and unwelcome in their home just because they speak a different language, have diverse cultural or religious practices, or because they were born outside our borders betrays the founding principles of our nation, which afford us freedom of speech and belief. While *Home* doesn't advocate for a specific policy proposal, it advances a resounding message: to keep our hearts and minds open. It's our hope that by reading these poems and listening to the accompanying songs, you will be reminded of the value of immigrants and the importance of making our friends, family members, neighbors, and fellow citizens feel welcome and at home.

We chose the title *Home: Where Everyone Is Welcome* for this very reason. Quite naturally, most people identify home with a place, whether it's a one-room apartment in a concrete edifice in Red Hook, Brooklyn, or a rustic Victorian in

Readlyn, Iowa. Home is the place where you live, separate from the outside world, where you can refresh, recharge, and rejuvenate. Just as a medicine cabinet may offer insight into your health or a shelf of books might reveal your level of education, a home can act as a window into your aesthetics, sensibilities, and even values and principles. It follows that if we think of home as a city, state, and country, we want them to reflect who we are as well. We must then ask ourselves what sort of place we want home to be.

At the same time, home isn't just a physical location. It's a sense of safety and security. It's a feeling of comfort and ease, familiarity and intimacy. Home is where you belong, where you are at liberty to think your thoughts, express yourself, and be yourself. You get this sense of belonging in your own dwelling, but you can also feel it when you're with dear friends, loving family, and genial neighbors. In this way, home may be less a product of your physical whereabouts than a state of being and creation of consciousness, activated by memory and the emotional centers of your brain. If you're at home in your thoughts and have peace of mind, you're in a better position to radiate warmth, friendship, generosity, and empathy to others. By being at home, we help others feel at home.

Indeed, home isn't just a feeling we *get*: it's also a feeling we *give*. As Americans, we must relearn this lesson, because immigration is not only the topic du jour but also the topic of almost every generation. The scourge of intolerance has been faced by many: Native Americans, African Americans, German Americans, Irish Americans, Italian Americans,

Chinese Americans, Japanese Americans, Mexican Americans, Muslim Americans, and so on. Such discrimination has been institutionalized: the Constitution prevented African Americans from gaining citizenship until the Fourteenth Amendment was ratified in 1868, and prevented women from exercising their right to vote until the Nineteenth Amendment was ratified in 1920. The Chinese Exclusion Act of 1882 prohibited Chinese people from becoming citizens; the Immigration Act of 1917 established a literacy test and banned all immigrants who came from Asia; the Emergency Quota Act of 1921 favored immigrants from northern European countries; and Executive Order 13769 and Executive Order 13780, issued in 2017 but stymied by the courts, reduced the number of refugees who can enter the United States, imposed a travel ban on immigrants from certain countries, and if upheld, may establish a precedent for preventing those from an entire religion from entering. Undeniably, these measures stoke anxiety and xenophobia, which create a cycle of doubt and distrust among Americans. This is America at its worst.

. . .

Immigration is deeply personal to us: Deepak is an immigrant, and Kabir is the son of immigrants. Our music collaborator, Paul Avgerinos, is also the son of an immigrant. Many guest musicians on the album are immigrants and first-generation Americans as well. You could say that *Home* was made by people who love America: immigrants and their children.

Deepak was born in New Delhi, India, in 1946. He moved to the United States in July of 1970 to pursue advanced medical training. At the time, the United States was still in the throes of the Vietnam War. The country was experiencing a shortage of doctors, so its hospitals and medical facilities were actively hiring foreign-born physicians. Yet India didn't want its best and brightest leaving the country, so it prohibited its citizens from taking the test required of foreign doctors by American institutions. To circumvent this prohibition, Deepak traveled to Sri Lanka to take the exam, which he passed. Because India limited the amount of money that could be taken outside the country, he left his homeland with just eight dollars in his pocket. With the help of an American charitable organization that recruited foreign doctors for regional hospitals, Deepak ended up as an emergency-room intern at Muhlenberg Hospital in Plainfield, New Jersey, where he worked with every type of patient, including those who had sustained gunshot wounds. In 1971, he and his wife, Rita, moved to the Jamaica Plain neighborhood of Boston, where he began a residency in endocrinology and internal medicine at the Lahey Clinic. To supplement his income, he also worked in the emergency room of a local medical facility for four dollars an hour. He later worked at the Boston VA hospital, where his hours stretched over long days and nights. Deepak knew that despite his and Rita's difficult circumstances, he wanted to be in America because it's a place where people can be free. When Rita became pregnant, they couldn't afford to have the baby in Boston, because her pregnancy was deemed a preexisting condition by their insurance company, so she traveled to India, where their baby was delivered, and Deepak remained in the United States where he continued to work long hours so he could provide resources to his family.

Deepak became a US citizen in 1984 and, with his family, moved back to Boston, where he served as the chief of staff at New England Memorial Hospital. He left this position in the mid-1980s to blaze his own trail, first as a representative of the Transcendental Meditation movement and later, in 1993, as the founder, with Dr. David Simon, of the Chopra Center for Wellbeing. Since 1986 he has written more than eighty-five books and has become a leading figure in the fields of personal transformation and integrative medicine.

Among the many honors that Deepak has received is the Ellis Island Medal of Honor, which recognizes individuals who have contributed to America by sharing with those less fortunate. Deepak feels grateful for America and believes that it isn't just a country—it's also an idea. We can't lose faith in this idea, because then, like a flame, it will flicker and burn out for all of us. People can climb the ladder here and succeed beyond anything they could have imagined, but immigration is what makes this idea sustainable. If we turn against immigrants, we turn against each other and against America itself. Deepak likes to tell people that he is Indian by birth and American by choice.

Kabir's father, Raghbir, was born in Moradabad, India. Wanting Raghbir to receive a better education and not having the means, his mother sold her jewelry to pay his airfare to the West when he was seventeen (the original plan was to travel by boat, but the Suez Canal was blockaded at the time). When he arrived at Palam Airport, in New Delhi, his suitcase was eighteen pounds overweight. He couldn't afford to pay the fee for the extra weight, so he went into the airport bathroom and put on eighteen pounds of clothes! When the plane stopped for refueling and cleaning in Khartoum, Sudan, where it was 118 degrees Fahrenheit, all the passengers were ordered off the plane. The flight attendant advised Raghbir that he could take off the extra clothes, and he quickly obliged. He finally arrived in Birmingham, England, and worked as a machinist at a Goodyear tire factory. His supervisor instructed him to ensure that no manufacturing scraps remained on the floor after his shift, so Raghbir organized his fellow workers into a team that kept the factory clean. They earned the factory's "good housekeeping award," a recognition that he treasures to this day.

Raghbir saved his money and bought a ticket aboard the RMS *Queen Elizabeth*, which was headed to New York City, where he arrived in 1960. From there he took a Greyhound bus to Birmingham, Alabama, to enroll at the institution that became Auburn University. He showed up as a brown man with a funny accent in the segregated South. Yet Americans made him feel welcome, and he was honored to have a new home. He proudly became an American citizen in the early 1970s. He traveled back to India to marry his wife, Surishtha, and they returned to the United States to start a new life. He began working at a small engineering company, and he eventually became its CEO, turning the firm into an international organization with sixty offices in the United

States and additional offices in nineteen countries. He later served as the commissioner of industry, trade, and tourism for the state of Georgia. Kabir's mother began her career by teaching psychology at a community college and later at a large university in Atlanta. She now writes children's books about Indian culture. She became a US citizen in the early 1990s. Kabir knows that America gave his parents the opportunity of a lifetime as well as new lives. They are proud Americans.

Paul's father, Constantinos, or Costas, was born on the Greek island of Kefalonia. He grew up reading Homer's *Odyssey* and was inspired to one day go on his own journey abroad. With an aptitude for mechanical engineering, Costas traveled to Athens, where he worked as a mechanic during the day and attended school at night. After receiving his diploma, he was hired to work on the freighter *Nicholas D.L.*, bound for Portland, Oregon. When the ship was passing through the Panama Canal, Costas developed appendicitis. The ship's captain prevented Costas from receiving medical attention, fearing that his new engineer would choose not to return to duty. When the ship docked at Portland on September 2, 1939, at the outset of World War II, Costas sought refuge at the home of his younger sister, who lived in Oakland, California. In a twist of fate, the *Nicholas D.L.* was later sunk by a German submarine. Young Costas moved to Rhode Island and eventually to Connecticut to join the defense industry. In Rhode Island, he met his wife, Juliana Peripoli, outside a movie theater. Her family had fled Italy before World War I, just one generation earlier. The United States was a refuge for Paul's parents, and he feels that he owes his very existence to them and the great country where they settled.

. . .

Home is a collection of thirty-four poems and twelve songs inspired by immigrants who have made significant contributions to the United States. We picked a diverse group of immigrants, taking their gender, religion, profession, and country of origin into account. We use the term "immigrant" loosely, and have in some cases written poems and composed songs that honor the parents or children of immigrants, or those who were or are visitors to our country. Because immigration is so personal for us, we wrote poems to honor the fathers of Deepak ("Father"), Kabir ("Home"), and Paul ("Odyssey"). Our choices aren't wholly representative of each category of immigrants that has enriched our country. But we hope our choices reflect the many roads that lead to America—roads that, we expect, will continue to converge, building the highway to our future.

We chose to write poems instead of prose because poetry has a lyrical quality that captures the *feeling* of home better than plain narrative can. It's this welcoming feeling that we wish would inform our cultural conversation and enhance our national dialogue. Some of these poems are biographical, and others draw on archetypes to express the essence of each inspiring figure.

In addition, working with Paul, we wanted to create music from these poems. Not only are Deepak, Kabir, and Paul immigrants or the sons of immigrants, we're also artists. We identify with what John Adams once observed: "I must study Politicks and War that my sons may have the liberty to study Mathematicks...My sons ought to study Mathematicks...Commerce and Agriculture, in order to give their children a right to study Painting, Poetry, Musick..." In short, our parents practiced science, engineering, and commerce so that we could pursue careers in which we explore our creativity. And for that we're eternally grateful.

As a result of our exploration, we turned twelve of these poems into songs because music takes us to a place that words alone cannot. These tracks aren't just about other people. They also can serve as your own personal meditations on home, transporting you to a place or state of being where you feel most welcome. Only by feeling at peace and at home ourselves can we radiate this feeling to our brothers and sisters.

We hope these poems and songs will help brighten the light and open the door. And that *Home* will provide a stronger sense of welcome and belonging for everyone.

—Deepak Chopra and Kabir Sehgal
May 2017

POEMS

BORDER

Inspired by Reyna Grande

destroyed bar**b**
erased palazz**o**
slackened borde**r**
toppled ryn**d**
razed edific**e**
obliterated retaine**r**
yanked lock**s**

fizzled grie**f**
abolished myopi**a**
lapsed tectoni**c**
left stigmat**a**
expunged callouse**d**
nicked intransigenc**e**

oxygenated room
persuaded digerati
educated brain
naturalized friend

primed you
embraced citizen
accorded shanti
championed futurist
enjoyed comity

SURVIVOR

Inspired by William Jimeno

Tragedy begets resilience.
When attacked,
we ask what can we do for each other,
and in these times,
character is tested,
greatness revealed.

Trapped, sealed,
concealed, covered,
screened, masked,
buried under concrete
and metal, as a friend
tries to rescue his mates
but is felled by the
surrounding destruction
and jokes with his
sergeant about taking his final
break from duty, firing
one last round into the air:

"Don't forget that I tried to save you."
Heroes and patriots,
bruised and cut,
yet calmed,
commonality, humanity,
brotherhood, sisterhood,

love at darkest hour.
Armed, geared, ready,
racing toward inferno:
"It's going to be a long day.
But we are going to get a lot of
people home."

QUEEN

Inspired by Celia Cruz

Sing through home,
Sing with home.

Wood doesn't rot
When it's from a spot,
Those Havana trees
Kissed Malecón breeze.
Two pegged bricks:
Cuban chopsticks.

Sing of home,
Sing for home.

Found the key,
Sliced the seas,
Shipyard born,
Blasted horn,
No ring, no shine,
These two blocks,
Tumba over spine:

¡Click, click / tock, tock, tock!
¡Click, click / tock, tock, tock!
.. ..
.. ..
Swaaaaaay. Swaaaaaay.

¡Click, click / tock, tock, tock!
Swaaaaaay. Swaaaaaay.

Sing in home,
Sing like home.

Can you hear the silence tonight?
Amid the eighths, out of sight.
Dusk falls, its blackened shade,
Twinkle, twinkle, wondrous star made:

Azúcar Antares,
Bachata Bellatrix,
Guaracha Gatria,
Punta Polaris,
Rumba Rigel,
Salsa Sargas,
Tango Taygeta.

Sing from home,
Sing past home.

Queen of song taps tonight,
Clave-wielding galloping knights,
Toward the distant Bronx crown,
Until their town becomes our town.

Sing as home,
Sing us home.

VOICE
Inspired by Joni Mitchell

Who gave you your kindred,
familiar voice that whispered
and whistled over the stereo,
as you crooned an American
bolero?

What sound does it make
when you touch pen to paper,
drawing vowels,
curving consonants,
bending phrases,
and conjuring argots?

Where did you learn
to tame the tiger
with no apologies
as you hailed
a Big Yellow Taxi
and set your course
on Harlem in Havana?

When did you ask
to play with Jaco and Pat,
and paint Graham and Miles,

and ponder
the color of melody,
the harmony of canvas?

Why did the summer lawns
hiss at you as the glancing sun
shone upon those
stepping to
the Boho Dance?

How do you lift words
from script and sketch
to track and tune,
from document and draft
to song and solo?

MOONFLOWER

Inspired by Carlos Santana

Welcome, flame-sky,
Mother Africa,
Mother Earth,
fusion worlds,
experimental transcendence.
Day dreamer,
night bloomer.

Going home,
Coltrane's altar,
cosmic ritual,
soul sacrifice,
spirituality awakens,
manifold mariachis,
velvet violins,
busking at Woodstock,
aglow with Havana's Moon.

Rock. Rock.
Let children play
with Tijuana tambourines.

I'll be waiting.
Somewhere in heaven,
with an open invitation,
jam session festivals with
the Supernatural.

COMPASS

Inspired by Chimamanda Ngozi Adichie

Not every story lies,
but some do, those written
with simple unimaginative
observations by the uninitiated,
who reduce a multithreaded
culture into a single yarn
that is repeated
and repeated
until it grows like a weed
into our collective consciousness
as an unshakable fact:
complexity begets perplexity,
depiction knives contradiction.

Not every African struggles so
Not every African lives in Africa
Not every Mexican emigrates so
Not every Mexican labors in fields
Not every Indian studies so
Not every Indian works in hospitals
Not every girl cooks so
Not every girl falls in love.

Maybe and perhaps
pen and sword
silence and golden

gray and grayer
bolt and bolt
buckle and buckle
you and me.

Stories with texture
pluck mangoes from sugar maples,
paste lingonberry jam on tamales,
curry garam masala with otoro,
coat Pop-Tarts with Vegemite,
groove timbao in Tehran markets,
dance Nihon buyo in Baton Rouge,
stitch batik into closets of Spanx,
carve baseball bats into Estadio Latinoamericano,
navigate freedom amid repression,
trace love along the contours of hate.

The world isn't tidy,
so give us your stories
that don't make sense
and confuse with
jangled and mangled
prose and poetry,
compass needle always
pointing true.

HANDS

Inspired by Hend al-Mansour

Memorized lines of math and medicine:
((desired amount / available amount) × volume = optimal
   dosage)

Chanted assessments of cade oil and cardiology,
rehearsed scriptures of sacrum and surgery:
("I will prevent disease where I can")
Baked into the prefrontal mind with blueprints,
to formulate a design on the future:
("AutoCAD 2017—New Subscription (3 years) + Basic
   Support: $3,763.99 Advertised Price")

On this shore or that,
which unfurls a welcome mat.

A studied Egyptian
with a second act:

flowing pen of ink and curves,
cooled under Bedouin tents,
where chess players advance wooden pieces
and mandalas point the way,
in those tents we gather to dab henna,
artfully, gracefully,
on bridged hands.

CANDLE

Inspired by Kahlil Gibran

Tortured soul
Spoke to angels
Sparked fire of passion
Longings
Ecstasy
Suffering
Craving
Pain
Death, the gateway to life
Love
Letting go
Dreams
Bittersweet memories
Wisps of experience
Threads of desire
Spaces of togetherness
Winds of heaven
Rebel
Hippie
Lover
Smiles and tears
The agony and ecstasy
Love and addiction
Voice of conscience
Life extinguished
Delicate soul

A brief candle
Dark-lit corridors of time
Now here
Now gone
The fragrance lingers

LEGEND

Inspired by Shulamit Ran

Today is the birthday
of not person but people
who turn one hundred,
an indefatigable group
that whispers from
alleyways and roars
from thoroughfares
and stands tall,
without apprehension,
a cherished
symphony that calls
the beloved city
of Chicago home.

Only a grand master
could fashion the West Loop
with its tink-tink bells
into atonal chromaticism
and memorialize Old Town
from upscale to up-tempo
and capture Bucktown
with belief and ballad,
and turn spark
of hustlers and buskers
from idea to intermezzo,
and otherwise fix
this land and its
orchestral family
into the permanence
of Legends.

ATLANTIC

Inspired by Ahmet Ertegun

They met for sherry and sardines
at five o'clock on a summer eve,
to chitchat about the machinations
of ambassadors and apparatchiks,
who waterfall into diplomatic bungalows
on both sides of the Atlantic.

He whispered into her ear,
"If you think politics is mighty,
try music."
And she responded,
"If you think treaties are communal,
try music."
And their eavesdropper observed,
"If you think laws are forever,
try music."

A diplomat becomes an ambassador,
a cultural king who nourished,
his education and social sensibilities feeding
those who move feet
and fill hearts with
palpitations of drumbeats.

Ray Charles sailed the Bosporous,
Aretha Franklin cruised the Euphrates,
Ben E. King navigated the Tigris,
Otis Redding floated on the Aras,
Led Zeppelin drifted across the Göksu,
all—across the Atlantic,
right up the gut-belly of the
Mississippi delta.

When dusk became night,
their conversation turned
ever more philosophical,
waxing about a new awareness
of mores and urbanity
and how the blues should be
infused with turnarounds and walkabouts,
twisting around the harmonies
of Duke, Cab, and Jelly Roll.

He mentioned to her,
"Lead sheets are drafts of new treaties."
And she said to him,
"Call-and-response is the breath of rapprochement."
And their eavesdropper observed:
"These two are cultural ambassadors who serve not
    one country
but all humankind."

WHISPER

Inspired by Yo-Yo Ma

In one note is every note:
harmonic partials hint their presence,

opening frequency,
fluttering overtone,
fawning wave,
whispering fifth,
nearing shape,
shuffling note,
familiar textures,
particle clouds,
space loops,
cosmic swirl.

In one silence is every silence:
pregnant between quarters and eighths,
before fingers climb south again,
on an expedition
to the center of our souls.

In one current is every current:
emanating from the man with a Petunia,

horse-bowed strings,
acoustic stage,
blueprint borne,

observing you,
thumbtack-size,
hulking shadow,
bobbing heads,
ordinary Thursday.

In one vibration is every vibration:
echoing throughout
like dewy drops
in Monet's *Morning on the Seine in the Rain*.

HOME

Inspired by Raghbir Sehgal

Blood of Ganges,
Flow through these swollen veins,
Now dammed shut by the British Raj.
The Raj prevails, sahib-ji!
Yet the trains still don't run on time. They grooooooan to a halt.
A million dreams dead, an ancient land caged like tigers and
    songbirds.
No courtyards or graveyards for elegies unwritten.
But poojas of cremation alongside the stymied,
    swirling Ganges.

Go west, young man!
Sweep.
Fail your quizzes, tests, and exams.
Sweep.
But sell your rings, strings, and chains.
Sweep.
Go west, young man! To riches!
Free every pigeon, as eagles of possibilities take flight.
Sweep those factory floors: ten dollars—no more.
Board this plane, sail that ship: double your layers.
Avoid every fee.
New Delhi to New York.
Agra to Auburn.
Moradabad to Montgomery.
Birmingham to Birmingham.

Where the Greyhounds baaaaark their mediocrity and misery.
Where Jim Crow's noose hangs its history.
Black, white…and dosa-colored.
Sweep.

Go west, young man! To glory!
Where a new life begins unannounced.
Firm collar, pressed shirt,
Show me a dollar, stardom-wala,
Where the Mississippi monsoons lift all boats
And the grass is as sweet as chai.
(But don't rip open the tea bag again.)

Go west, young man! To thunder and bliss.
Unzip your dreams in this lush land.
Dream your dreams with a supple mind,
Watch your dreams with hawk eye,
Measure your dreams with an engineer's scale,
Build your dreams with crushed rock and concrete,
Hold tight on political chutes and corporate ladders,
Soar, soar, soar like Arjuna's chariot,
Maharajah of Marietta,
Guru-ji of Georgia!

Go west, young man! To your new home!
An Indian's thanksgiving for America.
Where neighbors become cousins,
Friends become in-laws,

And family is rain on a barren day.

FATHER

Inspired by Krishan Chopra

If awareness is existence
You have existed in me
From when I first became aware
And now
If awareness is life
Then you have been my life
Since I incarnated into experience
And now
From the stories you told
To the magnificent hero you were
I am
Because you were
And are
We exist in the awareness
Where I is thou
Thou is me
In every
Everlasting
Now

ODYSSEY

Inspired by Constantinos Avgerinos

Long after Trojan War,
but before world war,
he embarks upon
his own odyssey
to discover a mythology:
where you're from
matters less than
what you believe.

Protected by Athena's gaze,
Avoiding Poseidon's wrath,
he sails west,
where he disembarks
to find strength, health, safety,
and his Penelope.

IDENTITY

Inspired by Huynh Sanh Thông

A land conquered over thousands
of years remains a place
of distinction, similarities,
ethnicities, eyes, and tongues,
despite erased borders and razed
walls from marauding overlords
who snipe at rambling rafts of
freedom that float subtly
along the Sông Sài Gòn.

Even if bodies are bound,
a mind cannot be boxed,
a mouth cannot be muted,
a pen cannot be silenced
because history will
unlock righteousness and
virtue, just as the arc of justice
is as recognizable as sunbeams
on cloudy days.

Because the words of a poet
are caps and crests,
that imply deeper meaning
just as the music note
hides and discloses other more
frequencies and tones.
The poet's phrases have
an abiding sense of purpose:
even if they miss
today, they will strike tomorrow—
again, and again, and again—
on those that kept them
from using the aboriginal
six-eight couplets and the
native language of their
own identity.

ORBIT

Inspired by Kalpana Chawla

Did you stare into the steady face of perpetuity?
As you hurtled toward the distant stars,
which bejewel the blackened days-and-mourns,
and spurred wits to the skies with flashes of revelation,
above & beyond, over & afar,
from the electric ants striking to life
on a rolling wet ball of magnesium and aluminum,
suffused with heated and looped oxygen?

Did you touch the welcoming fingertips of eternity?
During your rings of severe adventure,
zipping over Boulder's labs & Arlington's quads,
Chandigarh's sector 17 & Sunnyvale's malls,
Palo Alto's flying clubs & Punjab's partition,
reciting Irving Stone biographies,
glimpsing a handsome print of J. R. D. Tata,
painting a memory of T. S. Eliot illuminated with
the flicker of All India Radio,
stretching your robotic arm to karate-chop the dark?

In those sixteen minutes, between life and loss,
when regal anthem bows to longing requiem,
don't ask such questions,
because when you're home,
the loving almighty is unmasked.

NEWS

Inspired by Nikhil Deogun

Truth obscured with
substitute, alternative
facts that turn
up to down
left to right
yes to no and
maybe to certainty
as calendar spasms
from 2016 to 1984.

Truth discovered by
intrepid, dogged
journalists who separate
fact from fiction
story from spin
and who half humorously
rinse elected
officials with
sterilized spotlight.

Truth affirmed when
latter-day de Tocqueville
who brings self-realized
mirror from
Calcutta to Columbia
files human rights injustices

and captains a
press corps that
inspects captains
of industry so they
don't capsize
the people.

CITIZEN

Inspired by Wong Kim Ark

What does it mean
when the country
in which you were born
no longer considers
you a member of
the family?

Are you a migrant or
an expatriate or person-
in-exile or refugee
stuck in a ship named
Coptic awaiting your
own fate?

Aren't you an
unassuming cook
who toils in the Sierra Nevada
born on Sacramento Street
to Chinese parents
who like your brothers
and sisters risks residence
when you leave these shores
wondering whether
you will ever see home
again?

When you left America
for a brief trip to your
motherland, did you obtain
the necessary affidavit,
photograph, and testimony
of a white friend to prove
that you belonged here?
Are you sure you were
born on this soil?

Did you become a footnote
and flash point that provoked
the high court to permit
you and those of your station
to return, upholding
upholding
the Fourteenth Amendment:
"All persons born or naturalized
in the United States, and subject to
the jurisdiction thereof,
are citizens…"?

Did you lose faith
in your birth country
after it asked
your family and friends
to build its roads and rails
and mine its minerals and metals?

WORDS

Inspired by Luisa Aguilar Igloria

Words bend meaning,
around hinges of reality,
confronting colonialism,
with heart-shocked pen.

CINEMA
Inspired by James Wong Howe

Behind the scenes of Tinseltown,
away from the spotlight,

are the makers, the builders, authors,
composers, engineers, masons,
architects, editors, blacksmiths,
mechanics, costumers, and
cinematographers who toil as
storytelling bits in the machinery of
moviemaking.

These makers advance technology,
formed out of mental
maps, to further the human story
so that we relate to each other
in new ways, and have our imaginations
enlarged, so that it's not a leap
to realize that a boy born to hardened
railroad laborers becomes a chap known
for softening his lens with silky
and smooth, bendable and ductile
effects, so that, even when the
films themselves don't speak,
he becomes the talk
of the town for making the bold
bolder, and the beautiful more

beautiful, and the smudges of
imperfection cede to the
escapism we yearned for
all along.

PASSPORT

Inspired by Fareed Zakaria

A man without a country,
   is a man with a passport stamped in America.
A man without a place,
   is a man with a home left in India.
A man without a prayer,
   is a man with a dream reached.

A man without a fortune,
   is a man with a scholarship banked in university.
A man without a specialization,
   is a man with a curiosity stoked to read relentlessly.
A man without a family,
   is a man with a mentor from whom to learn
   in his adopted land.
A man without a computer,
   is a man with a pen inked to create and criticize.

A man without a dogma,
   is a man with a mind launched to detect duplicity.
A man without a party,
   is a man with a presence asked to grace state dinners.
A man without a veil,
   is a man with a face bared to critics of all affiliations.
A man without a jumble,
   is a man with a logic cleared with accuracy and precision.

A man without a puzzle,
   is a man with a riddle solved.

A man without a post,
   is a man with a column read across the world.
A man without an app,
   is a man with a book browsed in this library and that.
A man without a film,
   is a man with a show watched inside the Beltway
   and outside the corridors.
A man without a muzzle,
   is a man with a booming voice.

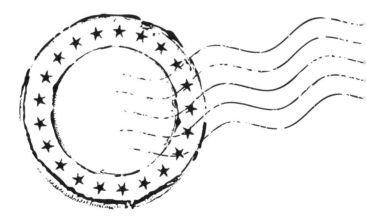

FLOORS

Inspired by I. M. Pei

Basement
A future starts
from the ground up
formed from
the Chinese soils
that birthed
a boy in a
high station.

Lobby
Who resists the
colossal forms of past:
French, Beaux Arts structures
that ossified the
forward march
of probability

Mezzanine
People not just scrapers
force heads upward-tilt
to today and infinity
like Le Corbusier
grand master who
moves metal.

Tenth Floor
A future realized
when mental scaffolding
of nerves and neurons
convert "What if"
to "Built to Last."

Penthouse
That beautiful glass
pyramid at the Louvre!
Who do you think
you are?

CAPS

Inspired by Elizabeth Blackburn

Tasmanian Angel,
divine messenger of truths untold,
hidden from the world,
revealed by
magnifying glass of mind,
telescope of soul,
microscope of body:

genes stored in
suitcases of DNA,
in the belly of a plane's
chromosomes,
coated with enzymes,
aboard a telomere of
insight.

Cell division,
clone precision,
foil elision,
cap provision:

snow caps,
gel caps,
talc caps
show patterns,

and models,
and outlines
of regularity,

sheltered by
the double helix
of infinity.

CODEPOET

Inspired by Sergey Brin

```
1   /* a basic "for" loop in Java that
2        enables computer code to be
3        executed in a repeated manner */
4   import java.USSR.boy.BigInteger;
5   public class Digital_Age
6
7   public static void Stanford(String[]
8        args)
9   {final int HisIDEAS = 100;
10  for(int world_growth = 0; world_growth
11       < HisIDEAS; world_growth++)
12  System.out.println(world_growth + "!
13       is " + Digital_Age(world_
14       growth));
15
16  public static int Digital_Age
17       (int Google)
18  {int progress=1;
19  for(int world_growth=2; world_growth
20       <= Google; world_growth++)
21  progress *= world_growth;
22  return progress;
```

GUARDIAN

Inspired by Mary Harris "Mother" Jones

Uncorked in Cork,
hungry for Hope,
O Canada, blessed are thee,
Chicago dress,
Memphis press,
resting and nesting,
with family.

PUNCH PUNCH PUNCH
to the gut,
this fever knows not husband,
or children, or friends,
but death, only death,
all is lost,
misery upon misery,
ghosts of despair.

Widow's reflection,
on windows of wealthy,
life anew in Windy City,
weaving garb.

FIRE FIRE FIRE
in the hole of city ablaze.
Shop-wrecked.
Vagabonding-purpose.

RISE RISE RISE
Phoenix Rising,
from bituminous mines,
dangerous woman,
five-foot giant,
Mother Jones,
face down power
with mops and brooms!

MARCH MARCH MARCH
O grandmother of all agitators,
strike out for fairness,
besiege the home of Roosevelt,
O guardian of children,
of men, of women, of workers,
show your jailed, locked hands,
force them to listen.

ACE

Inspired by Martina Navratilova

They say victory is sweet,
so how sweet is it
when you win
2,189 times?
Or when you claim
369 titles?
Or when you triumph
in 18 grand slams?

Do you ever say
"I'm sick and tired of winning?"
Because you make it
look so easy,
while others talk and talk and talk
about winning
but rarely deliver
an ace like you.

MAGIC
Inspired by Maria Goeppert Mayer

Dear Google Doodlers,

We write to ask that you consider featuring Maria Goeppert Mayer as a Google Doodle on June 28, her birth date. She won the Nobel Prize in Physics in 1963 for her discoveries and contributions to nuclear physics.

>> 2 ways to grasp the atomic nucleus: observe the particles or conduct rigorous experiments yielding rigorous data, of which you chose the more revealing latter method 8 times maybe you thought your shell theory lunacy unable to be tested by throwback instruments found in the stale laboratory's cupboard.

She helped advance the concept of "nuclear shells." Indeed, she knew that elements have a charge and that they have protons and neutrons in the nucleus. The number of neutrons can vary significantly, resulting in isotopes. She discovered that stable isotopes have a certain "magic number" of protons and/or neutrons, such as 2, 8, 20, 28, 50, 82, and 126. She also realized that these protons and neutrons spin like whirling dancers inside the nucleus. They spin in various orbits, or "shells."

>> 20 times a month you must have heard don't, can't, shan't, won't out of respect for your ascendant husband or elbowing men who skipped physics with their genetic shortcuts only to be tripped by 28 mercurial footnotes that wouldn't stumble you from discovering that:

The ramifications of her findings were significant because one could determine which isotopes were most stable and suitable to be used in the creation of nuclear applications, such as energy.

>> 50 is a magic number when the nuclei have said neutrons
which indicates a stability in the creation of certain elements—
it's magical because it's sturdy and strong just like 82 which is
an enchanted digit pushing us toward a new understanding of
the atomic nucleus as a shell in which neutrons and protons
get married and stay together in steady partnership

Her professional achievements are remarkable. And what makes her accomplishments even more noteworthy is that she stood out in a field dominated by men. In fact, she was often unpaid for her work and research and had to volunteer her services in the laboratory. As an immigrant from Germany, she helped her adopted country, the United States, by working in the Los Alamos laboratories on national security initiatives.

>> 126 is the highest charmed number deserving of the
highest recognition for your pioneering spirit: a GM unit
(obscure vanity?) or a Google Doodle (ubiquitous vanity?)
to remind billions of how you climbed unpaid and unwanted
in a Nobel manner, absorbing the photons of realization,
from the Baltimore classrooms to the Los Alamos workrooms
to your peaceful garden patch in San Diego

By featuring Goeppert Mayer on the home page of Google, you would highlight an important and overlooked historical figure from our past. Just the other day, a senior vice president at an American technology company was bemoaning the fact that there are plenty of jobs but too few skilled workers in the labor force. Now more than ever, we need to encourage more of our bright female minds to become scientists so they can be part of shaping a brighter future and inspiring sharper poems for us all.

FORTRESS

Inspired by Madeleine Albright

Across the azure Atlantic Ocean drenched in summer solstice,
Over benthic zones of life,
Mixed with sodium, silicon, and sulfate,
Against plunging breakers and galloping winds,
Upon lavish bubble corals and finger leathers,
Away from Poseidon's firm and resolute grip,
Under Titan, Ceres, and Europa,
By reflective beaches of mirth and hope.

An American citadel toughened by vesicular basalt and steel,
Chiseled from black gabbro granite,
Concrete blocks of confidence,
Wrought-iron balustrades of support,
Thick aged-oak walls of refuge,
Serene and secure sanctuary.

Unbolt the dead bolt,
Unlock the padlock,
Open the gates!

Fifty gleaming patriotic domes with burgundy and
    white stripes,
Gemmed chandeliers beam multicolored hues,
From twenty storytelling stained-glass windows,
On thirteen spiral staircases caked with purple starfish,
Hoof-clicked cobblestone floors,

Sunshine-soaked patios with cool-to-touch benches,
Cherry-marbled statues of gods, mermaids, and dolphins,
Glance knowingly at each other with familiar smiles.

Where friendship blooms like lotus petals,
Among all those shopping for wisdom at the bazaar,
And those with heads tilted up in the theaters of knowledge,
And those ambling gracefully under the pagodas of faith,
Or sailing in basswood-carved wooden canoes,
In the zigzag canals of devotion,
In the taverns of good humor and cathedrals of passion,
Seated on cushions of warmth and affection.

Where home is bejeweled with crystals and amethysts.
And the freedom to be beautiful,
In your own way.

REVOLUTION

Inspired by Igor Stravinsky

This piano, out of tune.
Whither the keys, or the room?
Play the form, nothing more,
Loneliness, he can't ignore,

Bloody Sunday,
Red Monday,
Mother Russia, lost your shine,
'Round the Bolshevik bread line.
Sunrise Lenin,
Sunset Trotsky,
Lausanne, peacetime,
Dawn of war,
Paris, springtime.
Dawn of war,
Los Angeles, lifetime.

Bended legs, rosined wrists,
Angular shapes, muted mouths,
Not a fairy-tale phoenix but *Firebird*,
Rising like a laughing comet,
Circling the navy-and-lime hemispheres,
Its tail illuminates dazzling path,
Twisting that century to this.

Over the restless audience,
Unto the adoration of the earth…eventually.
When winter becomes spring,
When revolution returns,
When the sacrifice of the chosen one
Lingers like a dominant seventh to the unaccustomed ear.

PATRON

Inspired by Helena Rubinstein

Millions and millions of pennies,
thousands and thousands of dimes,
hundreds and hundreds of quarters,
tens and tens of dollars,
accumulate like canned goods
hoarded in the run-up to Y2K,
but that bug didn't bite or
crawl into machines
and paralyze the grids that power
the robots that command artificial
wisdom and genuine intelligence.

So what of this trapped
energy of capital
and stale vigor of money
and its coiled potential
and all the lipsticks and
creams that it buys?

Wealth changes form,
like a chameleon, into paintings
and portraits, figures and figurines,
carvings that last forever or
at least until sun-beaten watercolors
lose resonance that evoked
brilliance that once caught
the eye of a producer

This his canvas on which we paint
noteworthy dead figures who
ran countries, marshaled armies,
and unlocked intellect, but
is green evident as blue and
coin as medal and sculpture?

Therefore the slumbering
money that lines pockets
weighs down feathers
like a colossal anchor
dug into the Pacific floor
with disregard and illiteracy
for the numbers of sanity
and alphabet of humanity.

INFINITY

Inspired by Albert Einstein

Spacetime asked matter to move
Matter asked spacetime to curve
Gravity asked bodies to fall
Black holes demanded stars to vanish

Is the moon there when none is looking?
Does the universe have many histories?

Infinity asked universe to expand
Cosmos asked consciousness to reflect
Mind asked matter to dream
Time demanded future to accelerate

Will mathematical abstractions obscure doom?
Is it too late for Einstein's nightmares?

Scientists asked atoms to react
President asked planes to fly
Nuclear asked bombs to explode
Waste demands morality to explain

Teleport me now
To another dimension
Away from
this junkyard
of infinity

RIVER

Inspired by Audrey Hepburn

Lush harps
Shimmering downstream
Gentle chorus
Among huckleberries
Flickering guitar
Serene river
Cascading violins
Under rainbows
Savannah drums
Ruby butterflies
Dulcet horns
Mandarin duck
Sliding brass
Painted bunting
Rippling snare
Summery wind
Fetching swoons
Rose ballet
Thin moon
Orchestral crickets
Cirrus clouds
Coffee sky
Clear moon
Infinity garden

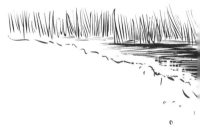

Fragrant leaves
Rustling creek
Apple kernels
Gilded aspen
Moist moss
Regal ranunculus
Triumphant tulip
Evergreen heart
Lune Luna
Luna Maan.

RECIPE

Inspired by Giada Pamela De Laurentiis

What goes inside
a melting pot?
Ginger, pepper,
dried beans,
guajillo chilies,
achiote, balsamic vinegar,
and mozzarella.

This pot will
nourish the fire
in your belly
and light another
in those hungering
for more.

BEYOND

Inspired by Alfred Korzybski

We confuse symbols with reality
The map is not the territory
Who are we beyond name and form?
Spaceless timeless dimensionless formless
Assuming form
Is the universe a human construct?
Words creating space and time?
Beings becoming flesh and blood
Secret passages dark alleys ghost-filled attics of mind
Disguised as matter
Korzybski immigrant from Poland
I wonder how many know you
Bamboozled by appearances
Limitations of brain
Prisoners of semantics
You pointed a way to truth
We remain busy
Asleep
Biological robots
Prisoners of convention
Perhaps not ready yet
The dream continues
Dreams images flashes of memory
Dominate our waking hours
There will be an awakening perhaps
To know that we are dreaming
Not knowing who dreams

BIOGRAPHIES
OF IMMIGRANTS

CHIMAMANDA NGOZI ADICHIE is an acclaimed writer who was awarded a MacArthur Foundation fellowship, or "genius grant." Her books include *Purple Hibiscus*, *Half of a Yellow Sun*, *Americanah*, and *We Should All Be Feminists*. She is from Enugu, Nigeria, and received a master's degree in creative writing from Johns Hopkins University. Though she's not technically an American immigrant, she is a frequent visitor and has made significant contributions.

MADELEINE ALBRIGHT served as the United States secretary of state from 1997 to 2001. She was born in Prague, which was then part of Czechoslovakia. She arrived in the United States in 1948 and became a citizen in 1957.

HEND AL-MANSOUR is a physician turned visual artist who was born in Hofuf, Saudi Arabia. She moved to the United States in 1997 to serves as a fellow at the Mayo Clinic, in Minnesota. In her art, she draws upon Islamic and Arab themes and aesthetics.

WONG KIM ARK was a cook who was born in San Francisco in 1873 to Chinese parents. Though he wasn't an immigrant, his story is important to understanding citizenship in our country. Upon returning to the United States after a trip to China, he wasn't allowed to enter, which set in motion a legal case that resulted in a Supreme Court decision affirming birthright citizenship.

CONSTANTINOS AVGERINOS was born in Greece and traveled to the United States by ship in 1939. He moved to Rhode Island and joined the defense industry. He later built a successful engineering company that employed dozens of machinists, draftsmen, and engineers.

He also obtained several patents for his engineering innovations. He was the father of Paul Avgerinos.

ELIZABETH BLACKBURN won the Nobel Prize in Physiology or Medicine in 2009 for participating in the discovery of telomerase, an enzyme that causes telomeres to lengthen and facilitates cell division. She was born in Hobart, Australia, and resides in San Francisco with her family.

SERGEY BRIN is the co-founder of Google. He was born in Moscow, Soviet Union. With his family, he moved to the United States in 1979.

KALPANA CHAWLA was an astronaut who died in 2003 as part of the space shuttle *Columbia* disaster. She was born in Karnal, India. In 1982, she immigrated to the United States, where she earned a master's degree from the University of Texas at Arlington. She became a citizen in 1991.

KRISHAN CHOPRA was a cardiologist who worked at the Mool Chand Khairati Ram Hospital, in New Delhi, for more than two decades. Previously he served as professor of medicine at the Armed Forces Medical College in Pune, India. He was also the chairman of the Heart Care Foundation of India and wrote two books. He was the father of Deepak Chopra and Sanjiv Chopra.

CELIA CRUZ was arguably the most famous female Latin singer of the twentieth century. She was originally from Havana, Cuba, and was prohibited from returning to her country after Fidel Castro assumed power. She became a US citizen in 1961.

NIKHIL DEOGUN is the editor in chief and senior vice president of CNBC Business News. He was raised in Calcutta, India, and moved in 1987 to the United States, where he received degrees from Muskingum College, in New Concord, Ohio, and the school of journalism at the University of Missouri, Columbia.

ALBERT EINSTEIN was born in Ulm, a city that was part of the German Empire. He developed and advanced the theory of relativity and won the Nobel Prize in Physics. He was a Jew and became a US citizen in 1940.

AHMET ERTEGUN was the co-founder and president of Atlantic Records, which signed major artists such as Ray Charles and Big Joe Turner. He was born in Istanbul, Turkey, and his father served as the Turkish ambassador to the United States.

KAHLIL GIBRAN published *The Prophet*, a collection of prose poems, in 1923. He is the third-bestselling poet of all time, after Shakespeare and Lao-tzu, according to *The New Yorker*. He was born in Bsharri, Lebanon. He moved with his family to Boston in 1895 and never became a US citizen.

REYNA GRANDE is an author who has written three books. Her first novel, *Across a Hundred Mountains*, is informed by her childhood experience as an undocumented immigrant in the United States. She was born in Iguala, Mexico, and moved to the United States in 1985.

AUDREY HEPBURN was born in Ixelles, Belgium, a municipality of Brussels. She was an Academy Award–winning actress who starred in movies such as *Roman Holiday* (1953), *Breakfast at Tiffany's* (1961), and *My Fair Lady* (1964). She was awarded the Presidential Medal of Freedom for her work with UNICEF.

JAMES WONG HOWE was a cinematographer who won Academy Awards for his work on *The Rose Tattoo* (1955) and *Hud* (1963). He used technological innovations to advance his craft, introducing more realism into films. He was born in Guangdong Province, China. He moved to the United States when he was five, in 1904, but didn't become a citizen until 1953 because of the Chinese Exclusion Act.

LUISA AGUILAR IGLORIA is an acclaimed poet who has published thirteen books of poetry. She obtained her PhD from the University of Illinois at Chicago, where she became a Fulbright fellow in 1995. She is originally from Baguio City, Philippines, and is a professor at Old Dominion University.

WILLIAM JIMENO is a US Navy veteran and police officer who survived the terrorist attacks on September 11, 2001. He was born in Colombia in 1967 and moved to the United States as a child.

MARY HARRIS "MOTHER" JONES was a community organizer and labor-union activist. She helped start the Social Democratic Party of America and organized many strikes. She was born in 1830 in Cork, Ireland, and moved with her family to Canada and then the United States.

ALFRED KORZYBSKI created the field of general semantics, which explores the relationship between language and its capacity to express thought. He was born in Warsaw, Poland, in 1879. He moved to Canada in 1916 and then to the United States.

GIADA DE LAURENTIIS is a chef and television personality who was inducted into the Culinary Hall of Fame. She was born in Rome, Italy in 1970 and later moved to Southern California. She has written several cookbooks and won a Daytime Emmy Award.

YO-YO MA is a cellist who has received eighteen GRAMMY Awards. He was born in France to Chinese parents and moved to the United States in 1962.

MARIA GOEPPERT-MAYER was a physicist who won the Nobel Prize in Physics in 1963. Her work focused on nuclear shells and atomic structure. She was born in Kattowitz, which was then part of the German Empire and now is Katowice, Poland. She became a US citizen in 1933.

JONI MITCHELL is a singer-songwriter who is one of the most influential artists of the late twentieth century. Some of her works include "Big Yellow Taxi" and "A Case of You." She was born in Fort Macleod, Canada. She is a dual citizen of the United States and Canada.

MARTINA NAVRATILOVA is one of the world's most successful tennis players. She won eighteen Grand Slam singles titles and even more doubles and mixed doubles titles. She was ranked the number one player in the world for 332 weeks. She was born in Revnice, Czechoslovakia, and became a US citizen in 1981.

I.M. PEI is a prominent architect. He and his company designed the Kennedy Library, the Rock & Roll Hall of Fame, the glass pyramid at the Louvre, and the Holocaust Museum. He is a recipient of the Pritzker Architecture Prize. He was born in Guangzhou, China. He graduated from the Massachusetts Institute of Technology with a degree in architecture in 1940.

SHULAMIT RAN is a composer and pianist whose *Symphony* won the Pulitzer Prize for Music in 1991. She composed *Legends* for the centennial of the Chicago Symphony Orchestra, and she is a professor at the University of Chicago. She was born in Tel Aviv, Israel, and is a dual citizen of Israel and the United States.

HELENA RUBINSTEIN was a successful businesswoman who started an international cosmetics company that was sold to Colgate-Palmolive in 1973 and eventually to L'Oréal in 1988. She was also an arts patron who commissioned work from Salvador Dalí. She was born in Kraków, Poland, and immigrated to Australia and, later, the United States.

CARLOS SANTANA is an award-winning musician who was inducted into the Rock and Roll Hall of Fame in 1998 and was named one of the best guitarists of all time by *Rolling Stone*. He was born in Autlán de Navarro, Mexico, and became a US citizen in 1965.

RAGHBIR SEHGAL is a civil engineer and business executive. He left India at as a teenager with ten dollars in his pocket and became a machinist at a Goodyear factory in the United Kingdom. He moved to the United States and became a citizen in the early 1970s. He eventually became the CEO of a large engineering company. He is the father of Kabir Sehgal.

IGOR STRAVINSKY was an influential and pioneering composer. He was born in Oranienbaum, Russia. His most well-known pieces are

The Firebird, *The Rite of Spring*, and his Symphony in C. He immigrated to Switzerland, France, and eventually to the United States, where he became a citizen in 1945.

HUỲNH SANH THÔNG was a professor, author, essayist, and poet who grew up in Vietnam. He was part of the Vietnamese independence movement. In 1948, after he was arrested, he fled as a refugee to the United States, where he attended Ohio University. He received a MacArthur Foundation fellowship, or "genius grant," in 1987.

FAREED ZAKARIA is a journalist and news anchor who hosts CNN's *Fareed Zakaria GPS*. Previously he was a commentator for ABC News and a columnist at *Newsweek*. He was born in Mumbai, India, and educated at Yale University. He considers himself a nonpracticing Muslim.

BIOGRAPHIES

OF ARTISTS

DEEPAK CHOPRA, MD, FACP, is an immigrant who was born in New Delhi, India, moved to the United States in 1970, and became a citizen in 1984. He is an American author, lecturer, and music composer who has contributed to seven albums and written more than eighty-five books translated into over 43 languages, including numerous *New York Times* bestsellers. One of his songs, *Do You Love Me*, featuring Demi Moore, hit number 10 on Billboard and remained on the chart for thirteen weeks. He recited Nehru's "Spoken at Midnight" speech on Ted Nash's Presidential Suite, which won the Grammy Award for Best Large Jazz Ensemble Album in 2017. *Time* magazine has described Dr. Chopra as "one of the top 100 heroes and icons of the century."

As the founder of the Chopra Foundation and co-founder of Jiyo and the Chopra Center for Wellbeing, he is a world-renowned pioneer in integrative medicine and personal transformation. He is also a board certified physician in the fields of internal medicine, endocrinology, and metabolism. He is a fellow of the American College of Physicians, a clinical professor of medicine at the University of California, San Diego, a researcher in neurology and psychiatry at Massachusetts General Hospital, and a member of the American Association of Clinical Endocrinologists. *The World Post* and *Huffington Post* global internet survey ranked Chopra the #17th most influential thinker in the world and #1 in medicine.

KABIR SEHGAL is a first-generation American whose parents are both from India. He is a *New York Times* and *Wall Street Journal* bestselling author of eight books, including *Coined: The Rich Life of Money and How Its History Has Shaped Us* and *Jazzocracy: Jazz, Democracy, and the Creation of a New American Mythology*. Among his other works are children's books he wrote with his mother Surishta Sehgal, *The Wheels on the Tuk Tuk* and *A Bucket of Blessings*. He is also a contributor to *Fortune* and the *Harvard Business Review*. A multiple GRAMMY and Latin GRAMMY Award–winning producer, he has collaborated with jazz artists such as Chucho Valdés, Arturo O'Farrill, and Ted Nash. Kabir is also a composer and musician. A US Navy veteran, he works in corporate strategy at First Data Corporation in New York City.

PAUL AVGERINOS is a first-generation American whose father, Costas, emigrated from Greece to the United States in 1939. Paul is a GRAMMY–Award–winning performer, composer, producer, and engineer with twenty-three critically acclaimed New Age albums to his credit. He is active in creating scores for a variety of television shows and has collaborated with Jewel, Run DMC, and Willie Nelson. Paul's multistep, intuitive creative process includes archetype and style-guide development, meditation, mantra, and prayer. He is a graduate of the Peabody Conservatory at Johns Hopkins University. He runs Studio Unicorn and lives with his family in Redding, Connecticut.

CREDITS

ARTISTS

Primary Artists: Deepak Chopra, Kabir Sehgal, Paul Avgerinos

Deepak Chopra: vocals, tanpura drone, shaker, drums, percussion

Kabir Sehgal: vocals, shaker, drums, percussion, bass

Paul Avgerinos: synthesizers, piano, bass, bass violin, six-string and twelve-string guitar, slide and volume-swell electric guitar, vocals, percussion, drums, sound design

Music by Deepak Chopra, Kabir Sehgal, Paul Avgerinos

GUEST MUSICIANS

Numbers indicate track

Andrew Allen (percussion) 2; Gustavo Casenave (piano) 2; Chembo Corniel (percussion) 4; Kate Dillingham (cello) 6; Lynn Yew Evers (piano) 12; Kevin Braheny Fortune (electronic wind instrument, flute, alto clarinet) 6, 8, 12; Juan García-Herreros (bass) 3; Steve Gorn (bansuri flute, clarinet) 2, 7, 8; Seunghee Lee (Sunny) (clarinet) 9; Ron Korb (bass flute) 9; Neel Murgai (sitar) 1; Mari Nobre (vocals) 4; Geeta Notovny (vocals) 1; Jeff Oster (flugelhorn) 2, 4, 7; Arun Ramamurthy (violin) 1; Mehmet Ali Sanlıkol (oud) 8; Amaryllis Santiago (vocals) 3; Gregorio Uribe (accordion & vocals) 2; Verny Varela (vocals) 7

Guest Choir: Nita Basu, Linda Duggins, Anthony Goff, Michele McGonigle, Carolyn Rangel, Felicia Rangel, Gabriela Rangel, Raghbir Sehgal, Surishtha Sehgal, Katherine Stopa, Gretchen Young 1

Executive producer: Kabir Sehgal

Producers: Kabir Sehgal, Paul Avgerinos, Jeff Oster, William Ackerman

Senior producers: Lawrence Blatt, Carolyn Rangel, Anthony Goff, Gretchen Young

Associate producers: Kenya Autie, Olayimika Cole, Laura Dickinson

Assistant producers: Lori Henriques, Armand Hutton, Rondi Marsh, Rafael Piccolotto De Lima, Eileen Sherman

Recording and mixing engineers: Paul Avgerinos, Oscar Autie

Additional engineers: Peter Karl, Kamilo Kratc, Charles McCrorey, Leo Nobre

Mastering engineer: Michael Fossenkemper

Liner notes: Deepak Chopra, Kabir Sehgal

Cover design: Brian Lemus

Package and book interior design: Cindy Joy

Photography & Videography: Yasunari Rowan, Brian Russell

Project Managers: Felicia Rangel, Gabriela Rangel

Special thanks to Jennifer Avgerinos, Herschel Garfein, Jana Herzen,
Ariana Pieper, Kashi Sehgal, Anastasia Shilova, Katherine Stopa

Recorded in 2017 at Studio Unicorn, Redding, CT and Hachette Audio Studios, New York, NY

AUTHOR PHOTO CREDITS

Deepak Chopra photo © 2017 Jeremiah Sullivan

Paul Avgerinos photo by Joe Frank

Chopra family photo Courtesy of Deepak and Rita Chopra Family Trust

Sehgal family photo Courtesy of Sehgal Family

Avgerinos family photo Courtesy of Avgerinos Family

AUDIOBOOK CREDITS

(Available as a digital download, sold separately.)

Produced by Kabir Sehgal, Michele McGonigle, Paul Avgerinos

Directed by Michele McGonigle

Recorded by Charles McCrorey, Hachette Audio Studios

Post Production by Michele McGonigle

Recorded in 2017 at Hachette Audio Studios, New York, NY